...sometimes I pretend to be a writer

Ben Shepherd

First published in paperback in Great Britain in 2009 by

Birds of Malta
PO Box 24
Norwich
Norfolk
NR2 2WA

www.birdsofmalta.com

ISBN 978-0-9562101-0-4

Illustrated by Mark Jennings
Cover artwork by James Ferguson
Printed and bound by Barnwell Print Ltd

In memory of Ben

Contents

Foreword

...sometimes I pretend to be a writer is the title of this collection, and I can't help thinking, I wish you had pretended more often, Ben, back in the days when I taught you poetry at the art school, where Elspeth Barker taught you fiction, and indeed I recognise one of Elspeth's exercises right there, in the book, because in the end you concentrated on prose rather than poetry. It's *A visit to my aunt* on p68: those phrases Elspeth picked out to use in a story. The wintery smile and the basset hound. I myself remember those because I might have been there, or maybe Elspeth told me about them. I suspect it was during that era when we team-taught. Reading the story now takes me back there.

Looking through this book, I can see Ben might have developed either as a poet or as a writer of prose. There is the constant sense of an incipient talent working away in both forms. The writing lands on the page naturally, with a certain grace. That grace is harder to acquire than one might imagine and still harder to develop and improve. Those who possess it to start with – though they may not always know that they do possess it – have, we would think, reason to be grateful.

Such grace is the product of a certain relationship with language. It is partly composed of a sharp ear, one that hears the roll or unwinding of a phrase or line, almost as it might hear music. There's little conscious analysis involved in the hearing: things just sound right. Or pretty close to right. And that, for a sharp ear, is satisfying. But it is not purely music. There is also a kind of judiciousness in the diction – the word-by-word sense of balance that establishes the range of voice. That too is generally impressive. If I slightly prefer the poetry to the prose that may simply be because of my own instinctive priorities, but I suspect it may be because the kind of judgment involved in setting lines next to each other is precisely the kind of judgment that Ben possessed.

Whether he writes in a form of lightly formal but pointed verse, close to song, as in *Bruised*, on p20, or in a fuller mode as in the Shakespearian sonnet, *Elements* on p27, or in a variety of free verse as in the lovely *Lights in the darkroom* on p45, there is an unforced ease about the work, something rather close to song. Song, I think, is the current that runs beneath all the pieces here. That is what makes for the ease.

There is also a desire to entertain that is most clearly evident in the prose which consists chiefly of anecdotes carved into a working shape. Some are funny, some are rueful, some critical: all are observant and lightly delivered, almost as if we were hearing them over a drink. They are a little like jottings towards a larger, ongoing piece of writing, a novel perhaps, filled with experience of location, both geographical and social.

Everywhere there is the evidence of a generous heart and mind. There is little personal angst on display and no cruelty, only a kind of wryness or wistfulness or ruefulness to give the light manner a proper ballast. But the ballast is reached without effort: it comes as part of the package, an aspect of the heart.

The fact is Ben did not pretend to be a writer. He was one, an instinctive writer at the beginning of a road he might have taken. It would not have been an easy road but he had the talent and most of the right walking gear.

Sometimes we are tempted to think – are sometimes taught to think – that only important books matter, that we should only spend time reading or listening to those whose worth has been underwritten by some esteemed authority, or by the authority of fame in one of its forms. We are, if I may take a geological analogy, encouraged to concentrate our efforts on a particular stratum of writing. I don't think that is right. Those who write well, who articulate their humanity with grace, are part of a larger and equally important stratum. They are important. They are good company. They are convivial. We stop to listen to them. They, through their words, present us with reminders of grace and loss and laughter and of the sheer fragmentariness of much of human life.

Ben's works are, unavoidably, fragmentary; but the best here is graceful, contemplative, convivial and humane – which is more than enough to love.

George Szirtes

I've thrown out all my toys and I'm playing with the box

I have become detached

I have become detached
An observer through the lens
Of a microscope
Familiar faces have become
Wriggling bacteria
In a Petri dish
Soon I will begin
My experiment

Rear-view mirror

Buddy Holly got into the back
Of my taxi today. Beaming
From a T-shirt, horn-rimmed
And handsome, forever
Twenty-two.

Mirrored in a limousine window,
Five o'clock shadows lengthen
In the ravines of my face.

I think about death a lot.
And sometimes I wonder, if
We'd hit that lorry
On our way back
From the Hammersmith Odeon,
Would I still be young?
My name written backwards
In the rear-view mirror.

The ostrich

Butter drips from clumsy toast
Onto the pages of novels
Bound by lust and yearning.
The dawn chorus splashes
Through an open window
Like the chimes of a rainforest
Waterfall. I travel widely.

Yesterday I drank myself silly
On moonshine with elk-hunters.
Before that, a wild sheep chase
Led me to the ghosts
Of dead friends. Far beyond
The realm of cathode-ray tubes,
Missed deadlines,
And overdue library books.

Today I buried my head
In Texas sand. Tomorrow
I leave for Nebraska.

And as they come into view

And as they come into view
Familiar friends wear out into
Strangers, refugees from
Private wars, armies fatigued
From passive aggression, silent
Breakfasts and bedrooms
Domestic attrition.

After wrestling (on the carpet)

I must have a word with you.
This is very sad. In Japan
We do not do this.
This happens once;
We invite you back,
Maybe in a few years. Twice;
Never again.

Pleasure is not limitless.

Loverman

I was all pissed up with nowhere to go

So I toyed around with the devil's playthings
I cracked my knuckles and I flashed my rings.

I'm a man of the world and I've been abroad
Where the men are all queers and the women are whores
So I gave them a dose of my true British beef
What a man's gotta do to get some relief.

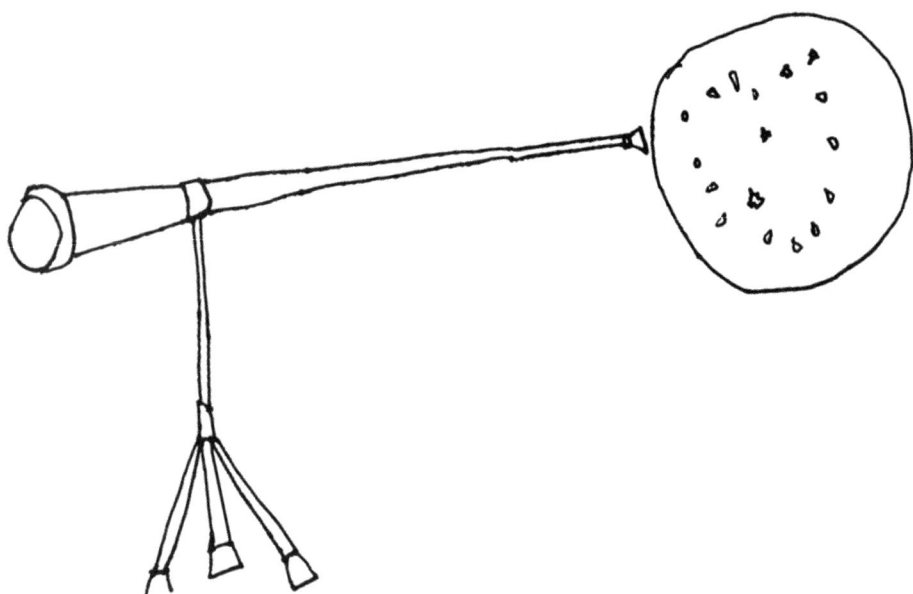

I have become detached

Familiar faces seem as distant
As stars observed
Through the wrong end
Of a telescope.

In darkened corners

The soldier, the sheriff and the sheriff's wife

Once upon a time there were two boys, one swarthy and slight, the other a strapping young lad with a shock of red hair, who lived in a village where they played, fought and grew up to be men together. They were also united in their love for the innkeeper's daughter who they would court together, though neither would take things too far for fear of destroying the best of friendships. Upon reaching adulthood they took their separate ways, the redhead seeking adventure with the army, while the other would eventually become sheriff.

The soldier was away for many years on campaign where he proved himself in battle and was highly decorated for his bravery. And although he would occasionally visit his old home, he was a wanderer at heart. During this time, the future sheriff kept the acquaintance of the innkeeper's daughter, and their love blossomed. Desperately wanting to marry his sweetheart, he was equally frightened of losing his oldest friend, but one day he found the courage to write a letter, requesting the soldier's permission to ask for the innkeeper's daughter's hand in marriage.

It was with more than a little sadness that the soldier granted his friend's request, but although he still loved the innkeeper's daughter dearly, he knew that as a professional soldier he could not give her the life she desired. And if the sheriff could, then how could he deny his two dearest friends the happiness they wished for?

The soldier returned home for the wedding where he made what was regarded as a most moving and beautiful speech before returning to his regiment. But as time passed, the soldier grew weary of bloodshed and the sound of gunfire, and left the army to return to his hometown where he settled down and looked for a wife, but with little success.

One lonely night he thought he'd go over and look up his old friends, but found that the sheriff was away on duty, transporting a prisoner to another town, and wasn't due back until the next day. He was disappointed, but the innkeeper's daughter invited him in for coffee and they began to reminisce about the old days. Certain things were admitted that had previously been left unsaid, one thing led to another, and they found themselves in bed together. However, it was not long before they were disturbed by the sound of the sheriff riding his horse into the yard, and the soldier fled through the back door.

The sheriff's trip had been cancelled owing to a murder in the town square, where a farmer had been stabbed to death and his attacker had fled. The two witnesses, who were both well-respected members of the community, said, that although they didn't want to believe their eyes, the red-haired assailant bore a distinctive resemblance to the soldier. After all other investigation had proved fruitless the sheriff, with the greatest reluctance, saw no option than to arrest his friend.

Although he denied having murdered the farmer, and later would plead not guilty at his trial the soldier, to the mystification of all concerned, declined every opportunity to give an alibi. And so it was with a heavy heart that the judge, who had known the accused since he was a small boy and knew him to be a man of integrity, put on the black cap and sentenced the soldier to death for justice had to be done.

The night before the execution, the sheriff visited his old friend in the condemned cell where they drank a bottle of whisky together, cried and bid farewell, one partly still bewildered as to the other's reasoning. The next morning he was hung upon the public scaffold, watched by the sheriff and his wife, and it is said that they never smiled again. It was a few months later that the innkeeper's daughter died in childbirth while being delivered of a stillborn red-haired boy.

At this news the sheriff went out of his mind with grief, took to the bottle and never returned to work, choosing instead to blow his brains out with a shotgun. And to this day, if you believe the stories that are told in those parts, and if you listen hard on a dark and stormy night, you can hear the wails of the innkeeper's daughter as she wanders the hills grieving over her lost boys.

Bruised

The scars on your face match
The scars on my heart,
Small souvenirs
Of why we're apart;
A scout's book of knots
We cannot undo,
That leaves us in bondage
Bruised, battered and blue.

Winter

Snowflakes fell from the sky,
As showers of plaster
From a collapsing ceiling
That crushed the bricks of shithouses
Back into the earth from which they came.
Sinking into the slush
That clung to my feet
I fell a little further down

Numb
Winded

I paused for a moment.
I saw pedestrians frozen in mid-stumble
Teetering on the edges of kerbstones
Some already with a foot forwards
Hanging over the abyss.

Discarded polythene bags
Tumbled and swooped in precinct corners
Dancing in the Arctic squall
Like acrobats
Or marionettes.

Reputations

This morning in a press conference
A grave face gave solemn voice
That Atlas was a drug cheat and a cynic.

More allegations on tonight's news
That Mars had faked his service record:
A national guardsman and a chickenhawk.

A court artist's impression of Eros, as he
Stood shame-faced in the Old Bailey dock
Accused of tipping his arrows with Rohypnol.

And exclusive to the Daily Star,
Venus exposed, an adulterer –
Though everyone said they knew that anyway.

Preachers and rabbis, imams and priests
All claimed that victory was theirs;
Guardians of the one true faith.

But in darkened corners I've heard some say
The crucifixion was filmed on a studio lot
Next door to Mohammed's mountain.

And the Ten Commandments were made in Taiwan.

Cold

In spite of the blazing heat, the terracotta tiles remained resolutely cool to the touch; clammy and inscrutable in a way that August could not penetrate. The agony in his stomach, and for that matter his left arm, he'd forgotten about that, had subsided to a heavy numbness that slowly, relentlessly crept across his body as he shivered and softly moaned. From where he lay, sprawled across the kitchen floor, he could hear the deathly rasp of the old man's breathing rise and fall in the afternoon torpor, receding with each breath.

The day had begun much like any other; nothing changed much round these parts. The pace of life around the rural market town was glacial, even slower than the wits of the locals whom he regarded with more contempt than pity. Old boys crawling to town in their filthy pick ups for the Friday auction, their dogs still filthier beside them. Sexless and hearty wives blocked what passed for pavements with their rough accents and stupid chatter. What a shit-hole. Yet, and for some reason he never cared to understand, people wanted to live here, wanted to move here from London in the naïve belief that it would provide them with a better quality of life. Tossers. Still, they were tossers with money to spend, tossers that needed to live somewhere, to buy ticky-tacky barn conversions boasting such features as paddocks, outbuildings and games rooms. Ticky-tacky barn conversions, which probably wouldn't last the next twenty years without being rebuilt from the ground up. Like he gave a shit. By the time those stupid fuckers realised how badly they'd been conned, he'd be out of there for good.

It wasn't really his fault he was here. Sure, he'd fucked up, but who didn't? It was just that he'd screwed up more than the others, and found out belatedly that old-school tie honour and loyalty counted for precisely fuck all when the ties were up against the wall. In solemn tones, the judge had stated that in the light of such brazen misconduct and incontrovertible evidence, there was no option but to impose a custodial sentence. No one had had the nerve to speak to him like that since school. Still at least that place had served him well; a taste for violence nurtured on the rugby field and honed in the brothels of Bangkok had seen him through all right. Got him out of there in one piece, not bloody and weeping in the showers like those other white-collar prigs.

Shit, it wasn't as if he'd done anything that anyone else hadn't done before. Granted, he'd taken risks, but he'd learned from his mistakes and could have put the money back twice over if it hadn't been for that crusading bitch of a journalist. What fun he could have had with that smug face. Didn't know shit about high finance, bleating about how honest working men and women had once again been betrayed by those who creamed off their labours. If it hadn't been for that dyke, they'd never have been any the wiser, watering the lawns and painting watercolours without a care in their tiny little worlds. Now they'd "lost everything" and they blamed only him, when it was their saviour who'd screwed them all over for a Sunday front-page scoop and a press award for her mantelpiece. Fuckers, the lot of them.

He'd done his time though, made all the right noises to the cons and the screws. Piece of piss, he'd made a handsome living off the vulnerable and greedy. Done it at work, play and school. Knew to make friends with the fat rich kids, desperate for acceptance. If someone wants something you've got badly enough, then they'll pay anything to get it. Money, homework, their bodies. The free market at its purest. He knew how to play the game. But now that he was out of prison nobody wanted to play it with him. Not on his side, and his calls went unreturned. He knew how to do his job, goddamit, but the ranks had closed. Too much of a risk, they'd said. Except the one he showed the video to. The one whose chubby frame shook with fear when played the grainy close up of a tear-stained face cutting to an all too familiar one, grinning atop a pampered body. A body that punched the air in exhilaration. That had changed his tune. Still told him that he'd never work in London again, but that the family firm of estate agents had a vacancy in some provincial backwater. So he'd kept a copy of the video for his own personal use. Still amused him now and then.

He'd been waiting to conduct a viewing of Orchard Barn, the orchard in question lying beneath the dual carriageway a hundred metres to the south. Only the steady drone of traffic penetrated the screaming silence as a blue hot sky baked the day into dust. That, and the crackle and crunch of a car pulling into the gravelled drive, as he stalked in the cool kitchen, a venetian blind casting bars of shadow across his crisp white shirt. Upon opening the kitchen door to the client, he automatically concealed his surprise at the tall, stooped man in his seventies, immaculate in regimental blazer and tie, campaign medals pinned to the left breast. Most emphatically not the city professional, self-made businessman or semi-retired criminal he had become accustomed to expect. And though he was fully aware of the public's contemptuous view of estate agents, the flintiness of the veteran's eyes made him uneasy as the taxi sloped off to whence it came. But he really didn't give a shit; if there was money to be made he'd take it off anyone who had it.

Besides, the coffin-dodger would probably be dead soon and Orchard Barn would be on the market again.

He gave him the usual patter, neither truth nor downright lies. The client showed neither deference nor cynicism. Please feel free to ask any questions about the property. You don't know who I am do you? No, I don't believe I do. I know who you are, you're Gareth Jenkins. Well, yes it says that on my business card. Great stuff, stuck in the middle of tractor land with a senile old git, with neither an end to the day or commission in sight. No, I don't think you understand me, you're Gareth Jenkins, I know what you did. I know all about you. Yes, I know all about you. Fantastic, how the fuck was he going to get rid of this raving cotton-top? I've come to collect my wages. Look, I'm afraid you've come to the wrong person, if you like I can give you directions to the nearest post office. Condescending as if speaking to a small child. I've come to collect my wages. I've come to collect my wages you, you murderer. Snarling. Flecks of the man's spit bounced off Jenkins' cheek. He recoiled in disgust. Murderer?

Murderer. He flinched again. Murderer, you killed my Mary. I watched her die of cold, I watched her lose the will to live. I watched her suffer as I watch you now, as you walk the streets a free man, breathing in God's pure air. Clearly unhinged. Look, if you don't leave at once I shall call the police. Yes, call them, and they should lock you up and throw away the key. Too bad they did away with hanging. Better men than you have climbed the scaffold. There's no justice in this world today. No justice, no decency. Foam flecked lips and crimson face livid against prim white hair.

Jenkins made a show of slowly reaching for his mobile, send this old fucker to the nuthouse. Best place for him. Remember, only invest what you can afford to lose, and the value of your investment may go down as well as up. He began to enjoy the moment. Perhaps a little too much. His guard dropped for a rare and fleeting moment. A swift movement in his peripheral vision followed by a searing pain. He twisted and lurched, clutching his wounded arm to his chest, staring in horror and disbelief at the ancient bayonet shaking in the old man's hand. You crazy old fuck. I've come for my wages. The bayonet thrusted again. Jenkins fainted, lost his balance and staggered backwards, cursing as his back jarred against the granite worktop and his mobile phone slipped out of his breast pocket and split in half on the tiled floor. His good arm scrabbled frantically for something to defend himself. Fingers clammy with sweat brushed, explored and finally grasped the handle of a small cast iron saucepan, deliberately placed to give an impression of homeliness and prosperity to the prospective buyer. A flash of inspiration. Fuck defending himself; he was finally going to kill. It would be a clear-cut case of self-defence. A smirk twitched his lips, which split into a broad grin as he swung the pan at his assailant's head. Although age had not withered the old soldier's resolve, it had gnawed away steadily at his reflexes, which offered no resistance as the pan swooped down upon his left temple and shattered his skull with a sickening crunch. For a moment he remained upright, claret streaming down his ruined face, eyes bulging with astonishment and fury before his body pitched forward, still gripping the bayonet, which split Jenkins' stomach open as if it was a meat pie.

As the old man's body collapsed upon the floor with a ghastly sigh, Jenkins reeled around, dropping the saucepan which shattered the terracotta tiles like so much toffee. Doubled over, arms clutched to his stomach in a vain attempt to stuff his intestines back into his body, he slumped down upon the cold clay. Outside, and far above Orchard Barn, far above the brilliant yellow of the rape fields, a buzzard stiffened its wings as it soared the thermals in search of an elusive prey.

Elements

You fall upon me in this arid place
And fast relieve me of my dusty coat,
Raining sweet kisses on my sunburned face
Before you slake the thirst in my parched throat.

The anvil drops and cumulonimbus
Darkened wild skies discharge a howling gale
That lashes my cheeks with cloudburst fingers;
I turn them leeward to no avail.

And then with frosty sulk you turn your back;
Implacable, glacial and opaque.
I search in vain for any sign of cracks,
Neither warmth nor kindness penetrate

'Til the gentle thaw when teardrops spring
And I'll forgive you almost anything.

Anne

I awoke to stillness, one of those hushed days where the volume has been turned down to a barely perceptible murmur, where one has to hold one's breath and strain the ears in order to catch the merest hint of birdsong or rumble of traffic on the London road. For how long had I been here, I wondered? My surroundings seemed at once to be both alien and yet familiar, as if a fading memory of times past. A room in a small private hospital, all pristine white walls and bed linen, the walls hung with reproductions of the impressionists lit by a pale sun that peeped in through venetian blinds. I remembered why I was there, that was certain. I had come down with a fever on the August bank holiday, and when it had failed to subside by Wednesday the doctor had been called and ordered me at once into hospital.

The intervening weeks had passed in fitful periods of sleep and hallucination, though it was hard to tell where one ended and the other began. Figures from my past, present and fantasy interacted as if characters in the same tableau. Kindly aunts with benign smiles metamorphosed into shrieking terrors and back again, unflappably resuming the ceaseless click-clacking of their knitting, and for what seemed an eternity, a ghastly shade seeped from behind the armchair and across the floor, a black tide that lapped at the sheets until it seemed that I would surely be drawn into it's desolate depths and drowned. Disembodied voices ebbed and flowed in the ether, as though caught in the static between radio stations. Through the interference came distant chatter in languages both foreign and familiar, a jumble of nonsense beamed in from a million miles away, and for one chilling moment of clarity, a voice of authority and the deathless words "she may not last the night."

I drank in the morning sunshine like a diver returning from the deep, nuzzling crisp white cotton sheets and exhaling slowly. I was content to just lay there, blissful that I'd survived the terrors of the abyss and that I could look forward to weeks and maybe months of rest and recuperation, a holiday abroad, maybe a cruise, and home of course, home sweet home. We'd made plans to have the Old Rectory completely renovated during the autumn and winter, so as to have it perfect for our silver wedding the next summer. I hoped that I hadn't been out of circulation for too long as there was so much to do, what with choosing paint and carpets, furnishings and bathrooms. But it could wait for a little while longer. So long as we got the kitchen and sitting room done before Christmas. That was essential.

Soon though, the novelty wore off and I became restless. The wall clock's hour hand had long since passed nine, surely the nurses should have long since come by on their morning rounds? That the curtains were open meant that someone must have come into the room. And although I was a little weary, I didn't feel ill enough to have been comatose and unwakeable at such a recent hour, unless I had made the most miraculous of recoveries. My curiosity began to get the better of me; carefully raising myself from my recumbent position I sat on the side of the bed and hesitantly put my feet to the floor. Straightening my body and testing my weight, I rose to my feet. Curiously, the floor felt neither warm nor cold, hard nor soft, in fact I barely felt anything at all. It was if I had been bathing in water that was exactly the same temperature as my body, a curious floating sensation that I put down to being ill.

Peering out into the corridor I could discern no sign of life at all, to all appearances it was deserted, a slightly mocking echo from the sterile white walls being the only response to my halloing. Even though my behaviour was highly irregular and it was certain to get me into trouble, I felt in great need of some fresh air after being cooped up in that small room for who knows how long. Opening a side-door, I greedily drank in the open space. Judging by the vibrant autumnal glow of the gardens, I must have been in that room for six weeks, maybe two months. But although the leaves had turned, the weather was still mild, as if summer could not bear to part from the world, the sun hanging weakly in the pale morning sky.

Encouraged by this, I took a tentative walk through the gardens, again feeling that curious neutral sensation on my feet, until I reached the edge of the grounds where they bordered onto a large field. Whatever crops had been growing there had long since been harvested, for it lay before me as a blank expression brown earth, ploughed in corduroy furrows. A flock of peewits scattered and wheeled across its stern visage, scavenging what they could before winter came, as a rook, sombre as an undertaker, picked its way between them. And at the other side of the field, perhaps a quarter of a mile away, I could see the distinctive two chimneys of the Old Rectory rising up above the copper beech trees. It may as well have been a thousand miles away, I thought as I stood there barefoot, my flimsy white cotton nightdress being all that stood between me and the elements.

Normally a cautious type of person, I wasn't prone to wild flights of fancy, but whether it was the illness or not, something had altered my psyche and I took off across the field in the direction of the house. My feet barely touched the ground as I practically flew across the field, leapt over the back gate and slalomed through the beeches before creeping stealthily around the corner of the house, feeling a flush of excitement as I thought of John and how delighted he would be by the surprise of seeing me alive and well.

I turned the handle on the back door and found it unlocked, skipping across the threshold as I called out for John. Upon hearing no reply I called his name again as I peered into every room in the house but received no reply. Having exhausted my search I sat down in the living room, after creaking open a window to let some air in, as it seemed rather stuffy. As I considered what to do next, I was struck by the absurdity of my position. I was long past breakfast, and I had evidently not consumed solid food for weeks on end, yet I did not feel in the slightest bit hungry. From where had I summoned the energy to run a quarter of a mile in bare feet across a ploughed field, why had no member of hospital staff stopped me? Curiouser still, my feet were spotlessly clean and dry.

And where was John? For a man of his fastidious habits to have left the house without locking the back door was unusual to say the least. I was pondering where he could have gone and for what reason he might have left in such a hurry that he forgot to lock up, when I began to shiver into my nightdress. At odds with the clement weather a damp chill was creeping in through the doorway, bringing me out in goose pimples. By the time I got to my feet and shut the door I was shaking all over with cold, and then with fear, starting as I heard a slamming behind me. I froze solid for a second but soon relaxed as I realised that I must have forgotten to secure the window on its latch and that the chill must have been no more than a draft working its way through the house. With a wry smile and a shake of the head I turned around only to freeze again, for the window was as firmly shut as if I'd never touched it.

Transfixed, I was sure that I'd opened the window and secured it in place, perhaps I was hallucinating again. But any doubts I had about my own actions were shattered as, hearing a faint clicking, my attention was turned to the hearth and, to my horror and amazement, I saw the gas fire burst into life, flaring briefly before it settled down to a warm glow. Letting out a strangled scream I rushed across the room and turned off the gas with shaking hands before collapsing onto the Persian hearthrug. Moments later, the clicking began again and the fire roared for a second time, but instead of a comforting and cosy heat I felt an icy blast that chilled me to the marrow.

Turning the fire off once more, I slumped into one of the pair of green wing backed chairs that stood on each side of the emerald-glazed fireplace and felt a surge of relief as the chill disappeared, only to be replaced by abject terror as the door into the hallway slowly opened and shut again. Picking up an ornamental brass poker from the hearth, I flung it at the door, where it gashed the white paintwork before falling to the floor, where it lay inert and useless. I then had immediate cause to regret my rash instinct when the door flew wide open again. I stared with horror and amazement as the poker rose slowly from the floor, and twisting in the air, hovered about a metre from the floor at a shallow angle, as if being brandished as a weapon by an invisible assailant. Swinging back and forth in a wide arc in the manner of a blind man's stick, the poker made occasional jabs before retreating and continuing its traverse. Then it began to move slowly in my direction, thrusting and parrying as if were in the grip of a fencing champion. A fencing champion, such as John was in his Oxford days.

Paralysed by fear, I could only watch as the poker continued in its relentless advance when a bolt of adrenalin struck me like I'd never felt before, not even when plucking our son Robert from the path of a careering London bus. I shot to my feet and, with all my strength, wrenched the opposite chair into a position between the poker and myself to form a shield. The poker stopped and resumed its silent hovering. Summoning all my strength I pushed the armchair across the floor, hampered by the rug that had got caught up in its legs, and with one almighty thrust I shoved the chair in the direction of the poker which flew forward and struck me a glancing blow on the side of my head before bouncing to the floor. Not pausing to check the damage, I pushed the chair forward once more, but could only advance it the barest distance before it met with resistance. I heaved again and, freed from the clutches of the hearthrug, the chair shot forward across the carpet in the direction of the hallway as I scrabbled to keep my footing. When I got within a yard of the door I was briefly forced to a halt again, and then suddenly nothing as the door slammed shut leaving nothing but silence behind it. Forcing the green velvet chair up against the door, I collapsed onto its cushions and wept and wept until I could cry no more before falling into sweet oblivion.

*

John Williams watched impassively as the removal man sealed the back doors of the second pantechnicon, turned around, and giving him a brief nod, crunched over the gravel to the lead vehicle and spoke a few inaudible words to the driver before retracing his steps and climbing into his own cab. As the diesel engine started with a reluctant shudder, the van followed its twin down the driveway, the first few flecks of November drizzle spattering onto the windscreen. Huddling further into his fawn trench coat, John took one last regretful, longing look at the ivy-shrouded rectory before he stooped into his gleaming German limousine and slid into the driver's seat.

The door shut against the mirthless slate sky with a well-engineered clunk as he put on his seat belt and turned the key in the ignition. Purring away, he paused briefly by the estate agents sign that now bore the word "sold" plastered across it in scarlet capitals. And then, with the barest movement of his handmade Oxfords, the black Mercedes surged effortlessly towards the motorway. Although since that terrible October day, there had been no repetition of those ghastly events in the living room, he had found that, coming so soon after his wife's funeral, he could not bear to live in that house any longer, and had lodged with an colleague in the city before he found a house of his own in the comforting bustle and roar of London, far away from the silent village, far away from the autumn that had killed his darling Anne.

My guitar has disappeared, it's sunk into the floor

A dime for the jukebox

I love rock'n'roll. I love the sound of a distorted bass. I love the tingle that goes down your spine when you hear an incredible song. I love the energy. I love it when you see the sweat fly from a guitarist's head. I love the firsts. I love the feeling of holding your first record in your hands. Love it when a band knows when to stop. I love the feeling of playing live. I love the journey to gigs. Unlike Morrissey, I love when my friends become successful. Though I feel more than a little envy as well. I love to see the steam rising from a crowded hall. I love the riff. I love it when a song encapsulates your situation so well that you can hardly bear to believe it.

I love the perfect chord change. I love the guitars that sound like an electric razor being stroked against your nerve endings. I love the sounds that bring me to tears. I love the records where you can hear the singer's breath. I love it when it makes you feel alive. I love it when a guitarist plays hard enough for their fingers to bleed. I love it when someone tells me that they enjoyed our gig tonight. I love it when you have to play a record ten times in a row because you're so damn scared of never being able to hear it again. I love hearing a good record for the first time in ten years. I love the anticipation. I love the sound of tuning up. I love the feedback. I love the sound of a phono jack being ripped from its socket. I love the crackle of old vinyl. I love second-hand record shops.

I hate rock'n'roll. I hate the skinny boys in leather jackets. I hate the artfully tousled hair. I hate the sneers. I hate the hyperbole. I hate the arrogance. I hate the cocaine. I hate the arrogant cocaine-fuelled

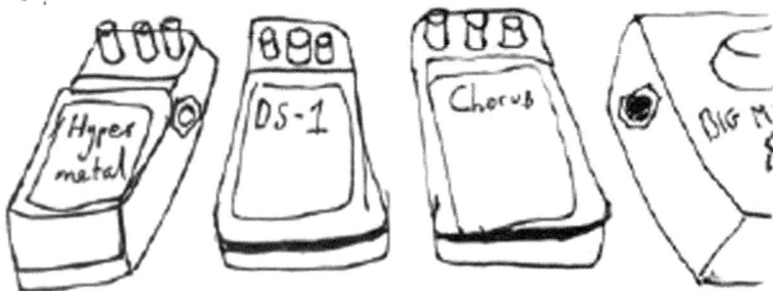

complacency that results. I hate heroin. I hate the celebration of the "elegantly wasted" rock star. I hate fakers. I hate groupies. I hate the musicians who abuse them. I hate the music press. I hate obnoxious sound engineers. I hate sunburst guitars. I hate the businessmen who buy guitars just to hang them on their walls. I hate revivalists that pass themselves off as revolutionaries. I hate the cult of youth. I hate the cult of death. I hate the cult of living fast and dying young. I hate the arse kissing. I hate the repackaged CDs with bonus tracks. I hate the drudgery. I hate the accountants. I hate the po-faced guardians of authenticity. I hate the haircuts. I hate the leather jackets. I hate the songs that are no more than a vehicle to the guitar solo that you see coming a mile away. I hate the autographs. I hate the riders. I hate the careerists. I hate stadium gigs. I hate the tour jackets. I hate the imbecile ironists. I hate the desperation. I hate the prostitution. I hate the "band as gang". I hate the drummer-phobics. I hate the miserable drummers. I hate those who whine when they're successful. I hate the smugness. I hate those who pretend that they're not able to play their instruments badly. I hate battles of the bands. I hate white people with dreadlocks. I hate the journey coming back from gigs. I hate name-droppers. I hate the swagger. I hate the stink. I hate corporate rock. I hate the chancers. I hate the businessmen. I hate the fact that I'd put my legs in the air if they would so much as blow me a kiss. I hate the poses. I hate the beatification. I hate the clichés. I hate the gratuitous string sections on the ballads. I hate musicians who are too drunk to play. I hate that "it's so bad it's good". I hate the rip-off artists who promise dreams but pay dimes.

I love rock'n'roll. When all is said and done, I can think of no better thing to do. Put another dime in the jukebox, baby.

The Top Ten

Ten strings
Nine A&R scouts
Eight in the charts
Seven inches
Six drummers
Five years
Four likely lads
Three chords
Two minutes
One-hit wonder.

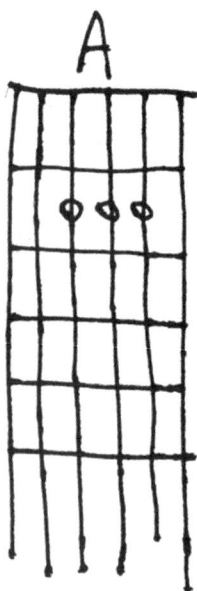

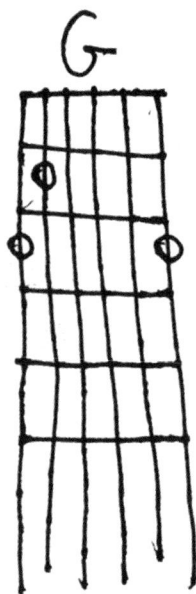

Coke

We are hanging around the bar when the Donkeys' manager turns to Rich and asks him if he can get any coke for them. Rich makes it quite clear that he is not a dealer in class A drugs, and even apologises for that fact, but the manager continues to press him for any contacts he might have. Rich has never had the will or way to buy cocaine, and explains again that unfortunately he can't be of any help regarding this issue. The manager says: "Come on, you must know somebody," which Danny and I find highly amusing and figure that he must have mistaken Rich's cold for something else entirely.

Finally fed up with Rich's stonewalling, the manager turns to the Donkeys' drummer and says to him: "You're from Norfolk, you have a word with him," as if we must have a similar attitude to 'outsiders' as the inhabitants of Summerisle, though admittedly by now I'm all up for building a wicker man in the beer garden. But the Donkeys' drummer seems disappointed that he gets no further with scoring drugs than his manager, and walks off in a huff. Fuck 'em. If you need coke when you're playing a battle of the bands, then you'll never get anywhere. Wait until you're successful to become friends with Charlie, and then you can stick it up your nose to your heart's content while watching your fanbase decline over a series of increasingly complacent and smug albums.

Chris

Rich calls me over and introduces me to a teenage boy that wants one of our CDs; I take one look at him and figure that he thinks it'll make him the coolest kid in sixth-form. Well, if he's anything like I was at 16, he will. But the merch table is folded up in a corner, and Rich tells me that Danny told him that he stashed the box of CDs somewhere backstage. I make out that I know exactly what he's talking about, then take a mosey down Main Street.

Denuded of its throng, the auditorium looks smaller and the strip lights do nothing to flatter its age. My footsteps fall heavier as I cross the pockmarked parquet then slip through a pair of grubby curtains, and its not until after I find the box of CDs hidden underneath two guitars and a duffel coat, and my eyes adapt to the backstage gloom, that I see him hunched on the edge of a chair. All about him is an air of despond, from the beer can in danger of falling from his hand and dribbling its contents on the floor, to the sullen pout most certainly not for effect. I rise to my feet, clutching the box of CDs like a babe in arms, and shuffle round to the right a little so I can look him in the face. He's nobody I recognise.

"Are you alright mate?" I ask, which is a rhetorical question if there's ever been one, for he is most certainly not. But I receive a reply of sorts, first a non-committal grunt and then a sigh. And then just as I'm about to leave him to wallow, but before I can think of anything suitably consoling to say, he ventures a question: "Do you know who I am?" But rather than the arrogance that tends to come with such a question, all I hear is a sorrowful plea for recognition. All I can do is ask him if he played tonight. He says yeah, I'm in the Wonderlust: the next big thing whose coat-tails we've been riding tonight, and three-quarters of whom are presently loafing in the bar where they are looking pale and ersatz interesting, signing records, chatting up girls, and generally acting quite the raconteurs. And then while I'm wondering why he's not there with them, and if their manager is still trying to score some coke, he asks me the question that politeness dictates should've been mine. What instrument does he play?

So I think for what I hope is an inconspicuous moment or two and try to be tactful: is he the guitarist? He sniffs a little and I hope that he's not going to break down in front of me. And then I feel like my guts are imploding and I think of Chris and that I'm going to break down as well. Mercifully he doesn't and croaks that he's the drummer and "no-one knows who I am". It turns out that after he'd packed up his drums and gone to the bar, he got ignored by all the autograph hunters and pretty girls, even his band for fuck's sake, and slunk backstage to nurse his wounds, wondering whether it was too late to get his old job back.

It happened a few years ago, and it happened here. At the time I worked behind the bar, and a perk of the job was free entry to pretty much any gig you wanted. On that day I cashed in my privileges and snuck in to see my friend's band who were supporting one of the bands of the moment whose single was a surprise hit on the radio and in the indie clubs that summer. My friend's band were pretty good, but the headline band were not really my cup of tea so I didn't see much of them, just a few songs to see what all the fuss was about, and spent most of the rest of the night in the bar congratulating my friends on their performance. Just before last orders, I went to get a round from the bar. My friend Jack was tending the bar, and as he pulled the pints he made a request. His sister was a fan of the headlining band and would I mind getting their autographs for her? He wasn't much of a music fan; rather theatre and cinema were his kind of thing. So he gave me a couple of quid to buy one of their singles from the merch table and get it signed. There was something of a scrum backstage, and the one female bouncer was having a fine time controlling it. The problem for me was that I had only a passing knowledge of the band and whereas the two guitarists were easily identifiable by their red and pink hair, the male rhythm section were rather more anonymous. The only thing for it was to go and ask every likely looking bloke, who wasn't either clutching records and t-shirts or trying to chat up the guitarists, and ask them if they were in the band. I found the bass player with little difficulty, and he was glad to oblige, but locating the drummer took a little longer. I was asking probably the tenth or twelfth likely looking chap when, rather than a variation on "Sorry, it's not me," he replied. "You don't know who I am, do you?" I didn't, and briefly racked my brain for any suspect who might have his business saying such a thing in such a place, and had to confess that no, I didn't know who he was. "I'm Chris," he said in a quiet voice." I'm the drummer." I didn't know quite what to say, apart from confessing that I was collecting autographs for the barman's sister, and I guess we both felt awkward but he signed the record with good grace so I thanked him and said I had to go now, and I left.

Two weeks later, Chris hung himself in his parent's garage.

Sad songs

Tell me your true story now
As the storms are closing in,
All your sacred that is profane
Every little lie you've been.
Exhale a ghost's lament
Of the wicked and the pure,
Croon a gossamer lullaby:
A dark night's overture
At 33 rpm;
Crackling static on a record,
A whisper frozen on the air,
A sustained minor chord.
I like the melancholy sounds,
Cry me a slide guitar
For listening to these sad songs

Never got me very far.

It makes me laugh, so that must count for something

Scenes from a waiting room

Scene 1

"Excuse me please Doctor, but how long will it take to be seen?"
"Sorry, I don't know. I'm actually a dentist."
"Really? Why are you at the hospital"
"I have a drill wound to the hand, ouch."
"Oh dear, that's rather nasty, isn't it? Sorry to have bothered you."
"No problem."

Scene 2

"Excuse me, but we've been waiting here for four hours. My daughter's burnt her hand and now my son says he's going to be sick. We need to be seen now, this is totally unacceptable."
"Sorry, but I'm actually a dentist."
"Never mind."

Scene 3

"Sorry to bother you. But the chap over there said you were a dentist."
"I am indeed."
"I have a terrible toothache, would you mind having a look?"
"I'm afraid I have a drill-bit lodged in my hand."
"Yuck, would you like a mint humbug?"
"Thanks, that's very kind of you."

Scene 4

"This is ridiculous, I've been waiting here for five hours now and it's bloody freezing in here. I've a good mind to complain to my MP about this. Fat lot of good it would do though."
"Er…"
"Well, aren't you going to do something about it then? I don't pay my taxes for you to sit on your backside doing nothing. The state of the NHS today, it's bloody criminal."

"Sorry, but I don't actually work here."

"I can see that you're not bloody working."

"Well I'm waiting to be seen too."

"Then why are you dressed up as a doctor? Bit early in the day for fancy dress parties isn't it?"

"I'm a dentist. A dentist who happens to have drilled a hole in his hand."

"Well you ought to be more careful then, especially with the prices you lot charge. It's a bloody disgrace. I wonder if you haven't drilled a hole in your patient's head. Probably charged them for that as well."

"I'll knock your teeth out for free if you like."

"You just stay right there while I call the police, I'll have you arrested for threatening behaviour. My son-in-law's a policeman, you know. Did you hear that everybody? He threatened me, he threatened to hit me."

"I'll make that a promise if you like."

"Just you wait…"

Scene 5

"Excuse-Moi, parlez-vouz Francais?"

"Nein. Scheisskopf."

"Pardon?"

"Arrivederci."

Scene 6

"Are you…?"

"No. In the name of all that is holy, I'm not a bloody doctor. I'm a dentist with a hole in my hand and as such I am completely powerless to deal with your enquiry. Having said that, if you're a tailor or seamstress, I'll fill your teeth in exchange for a few stitches. Otherwise, I'm as cold and miserable as you are and there's nothing I can do about it."

"Are you Mr Harvey?"

"Yes I am, and who might you be?"

"I am a doctor."

I like short poems

Lights in the darkroom

Quarter to three on a Monday
Afternoon watching the tap drip.

Just part of a project
To see if I could conjure up
A tangible translation
Of those erratic abstracts:
That spectral nebula;
Elusive in my peripheral vision.

I am a fisherman
Trawling for the moon in a duck-pond.

Student farce

CRO-MAG: (on his mobile) Speak up, I can't hear you. I'm in the post office. In. The. Post. Office.

SANTA: No shit, Sherlock.

CRO-MAG: Yeah, I quite fancy number twelve but I don't know, I could get a bit of number 14 too.

TRACEY: Chicken-fried rice?

CRO-MAG: This is my wife I'm talking about here, my future wife. Yeah well, I'll call you in the New Year then. Laters. (to Josh) You gotta love those Asian girls.

JOSH: Uh?

CRO-MAG: Asian girls, y'know. I'm thinking about getting one of those Thai brides. Mail-order like. I could go for one of those Asian women I reckon. They know their place, know what I mean? Cook your dinner; iron your shirts; do whatever in bed, none of that bollocks about equality. I'm a man's man. I tell you, the women in this country are too much bloody trouble. Not like those Thai girls, they don't even need a man to get them started. I'd like to read their book of tricks.

JOSH: Um.

CRO-MAG: Last time I went over there I took some of the old willy medicine along. You know, the old super V; the yellow brick road in a blue pill. Takes you all the way to the Emerald City where you can get as mad and bad as you like and you'll never want to go home.

JOSH: Er.

CRO-MAG: All night long mate, all night long. What about you? Got a woman then? Looks like you have to me, either that or someone's died. Ah, you don't like what I'm saying do you? Must be a new man, one of them queers. (to Santa) Sorry mate.

JOSH: Well, I've sort of got a girlfriend.

CRO-MAG: Sort of? How can you "sort of" have a girlfriend? You either got a woman or you bleedin' well ain't. Believe me, if you "sort of" got a woman then she ain't the sort of woman you want, know what I mean? That's the sort of woman who's too much bleedin' trouble.

JOSH: She's my penpal y'know. On the internet and that. I haven't been able to meet her yet. Well I'm flying out to see her tomorrow. I'm here to get my traveller's cheques you see. Oh, I can't wait.

CRO-MAG: What? She from up north or something?

JOSH: No, she's from Kiev, in the Ukraine. She's the sister of one of my mates from work. She writes me such beautiful letters.

Letter from Sonia

EN MASSE: Aaah!

CRO-MAG: I bet I know what Sonia really wants. Probably one of those gypsies, asylum-seekers and all that. Reckon she's only after you so she can come over here and sponge off the system. Ukrainian? Give me a Thai any day of the week. That's what it's all about. It's not benefits my wife'll be sponging, know what I mean?

BETH: How dare you! Talking about women like you're ordering a curry.

JOSH: (faintly) She's a nurse.

CRO-MAG: Thai actually. And I'll talk how I want. You some kind of dyke then?

BETH: Yeah, I am a lesbian, but so what? Firstly I'm a woman and I have to say that on the behalf of womankind, I find your remarks to be extremely offensive.

CRO-MAG: Thought so, I can tell you man-haters from a mile off. That your bird in the leathers? Cor, she can ride me any day.

BETH: Typical. Sex; sex; sex. Man want food. Man want drink. Man want fuck. Man want fight. Then man want woman to clear up after him. And you wonder why women might seek the empowerment of another woman's love?

CRO-MAG: Yeah, I do actually. How does that work, eh? All yak, yak, yak, and not so much as a hand-job at the end of it I reckon.

VIV: Sadly, in this case you're damn near right.

BETH: What!?

CRO-MAG: (answers mobile) Awright mum? (pauses) Sorry, hello mother.

Yes, I picked up your prescription, I'm at the post office now, I'm in the queue. (pauses) Yes, I'll be home on time. (pauses) No, I won't be late for dinner, bye mum. Sorry, mother.

EN MASSE: Counter number seven please.

VIV: Why does everything take so bloody long?

BETH: It's Christmas.

VIV: This queue is taking fucking forever.

BETH: Would you mind not swearing so much?

VIV: Oh, she speaks to me.

BETH: (ignores her)

VIV: I took the day off to help you with the shopping.

BETH: I didn't ask you to.

VIV: Well, I had to stop you getting more socks and perfume for my family.

BETH: I don't always buy your family socks and perfume.

VIV: You do, I opened the bathroom cabinet once and found four Christmases worth of perfume.

BETH: That's great, that's just great, Thanks for that.

VIV: Come on; stop being such a bore. Lighten up; I was only messing about.

BETH: Yeah, well. Whatever.

VIV: When did you turn into such a tight-arse? You're no fun anymore.

BETH: Maybe it's because I don't enjoy public humiliation. How could you tell that arsehole that we're not having sex?

CRO-MAG: Excellent, catfight. Yeah, how come you're not getting any?

VIV: Fuck off.

SANTA: This is why I do my Christmas shopping on the internet.

VIV: Look, sorry. I said I was just messing around.

BETH: Like you were just 'messing around' with Sophie?

VIV: Yeah, we were just having a bit of fun.

BETH: And her boyfriend? Was it 'just a bit of fun' to stick your tongue down his throat as well?

CRO-MAG: You can stick your tongue down my throat anytime you want, love.

TRACEY & STACEY: Eew.

VIV: (ignores him)

BETH: Well?

VIV: You're blowing this out of all proportion. Can't we talk about this in private?

BETH: Oh no, I'd much rather we had it out here. After all, you seem to be happy to have everything out in public. By the way, last night, nice thong, everyone else in the pub liked it too. Shame you didn't come home with it.

CRO-MAG: A thong and leathers? Come on baby! Come home to a real man.

BETH & VIV: Fuck you.

EN MASSE: Counter number five please.

SANTA: (offers bottle to Viv) You look like you need a drink.

VIV: Thanks. (takes a swig)

BETH: What thehell d'you think you're doing? You've got to ride your bike home.

VIV: You want to call me a whore, don't you? You want to call me a dirty fucking slag but you can't bring yourself to say it. You're so fucking uptight; we were just having fun. F. U. N. Fun. Sometimes I wonder if you know the fucking meaning of the word.

BETH: (sniffs and ignores her)

STACEY: Have you got my Primark bag?

TRACEY: Nah, don't think so, did you leave it in Maccy Dees?

STACEY: Nah, don't think so; oh no, it's OK I've got it. These trackies are mint.

TRACEY: Yeah, mint! This queue's not even moving – look at that sad prick.

STACEY: He's a right loser. Oi! Don't you know Santa doesn't exist?

SANTA: Sometimes I wish I didn't. The world's a bleak and miserable place.

TRACEY: You what? Did you hear anything? I thought I heard something but there's no fucker there.

STACEY: He's collecting for his own charity.

TRACEY: What's the matter, sicko? Want me to sit on your lap?

STACEY: Oh yeah, he's blatantly checking you out.

TRACEY: Why is Father Christmas a dirty paedo?

STACEY: Dunno.

TRACEY: Would you trust a man who sneaks into kids' bedrooms in the middle of the night and empties his sack?

STACEY: Eurgh! Shut up!

TRACEY: I fucking hate Christmas.

BETH: Would you mind not swearing?

STACEY & TRACEY: Fuck off!

BETH: For fuck's sake.

TRACEY: That was mint.

STACEY: Mint.

TRACEY: I fucking hate Christmas.

STACEY: Ooh, watch your language Tracey.

TRACEY: Oh yeah, fuck it. Christmas.

STACEY: You dick, what are you up to?

TRACEY: Going to my nan's.

STACEY: Fucking wrinkly Christmas for you then.

TRACEY: That's alright, she makes a well mint trifle. What about you?

STACEY: Dunno – my dad's gone chuffing cuckoo.

TRACEY: Not again? That's shit mate.

*** 'Anneka Rice' explodes onto stage in the way only Anneka Rice could do. 'She' looks out of breath, frightfully enthusiastic and a little flushed around the cheeks***

'ANNEKA': (thumbs up to audience) OK! Ready to roll? Fantastic – and action!

BETH: Excuse me. Where d'you think you're going? This is a queue. We are queueing.

'ANNEKA': Listen up! I'm Anneka Rice and today we're in Leatherhead, where the festive season is in full swing. It's that time of year when just about everybody is warmed by a wonderful sense of faith, hope, and charity. The decorations are glittering, little hands are busy making lists, and the cash-registers are jingling like sleigh bells.

CRO-MAG: Blimey, all I remember of Anneka Rice is a backside like a moose.

VIV: I don't think that's actually her.

TRACEY: Er…Stace, is that your dad?

STACEY: Fucking hell!

'Anneka', oblivious, stops talking, a contrived 'concerned' expression spreads across 'her' features while 'she' wrings her hands in a slow washing motion

'ANNEKA': Now, at times like these it's easy to forget about those less fortunate than ourselves. And I'd like to ask you guys if you're aware of a condition called A-N-U-S P-R-O-F-U-N-D-U-S? Let's look at this terrible affliction in a nutshell: it's a crippling disease where babies are born completely lacking any sense of humour whatsoever, and it leaves its sufferers unable to have fun like you and me.

CRO-MAG: For Chrissake, this chap's a little too involved, ain't he?

VIV: I'd say so.

a smile opens 'Anneka's' face into a countenance of horrifying glee

'ANNEKA': Now today we'll be attempting to raise some of your money to help a few of those with this unfortunate condition enjoy Christmas a little more. My challenge is to find out if any of these people in this queue are willing to write a cheque right here, right now, to the Guildford Hospice for the terminally pretentious. It doesn't have to be much, guys. Twenty; ten; even five pounds. We all know every little helps.

STACEY: Don't give him anything, whatever you do.

'ANNEKA': OK, let's go. Anneka Challenge.

JOSH: (pulls a crumpled fiver from his pocket) There you go.

'ANNEKA': Brilliant, that five pounds will make a sick child's Christmas dreams come true.

CRO-MAG: What are you giving money to that loony for?

BETH: He's not a loony, he's ill and needs help.

JOSH: (taken aback) Oh, I was thinking about Sonia.

CRO-MAG: I tell you mate, you're done for.

BETH: And you need shooting.

VIV: For fuck's sake, stop sticking your oar in. We're nearly at the front of the queue now so you can send off that parcel and we can go and have that coffee and talk about your precious issues.

STACEY: Yeah, shut up! Rabbit; rabbit; rabbit.

CRO-MAG: So much for female solidarity then, eh?

'ANNEKA', BETH, VIV, STACEY & TRACEY: Fuck off!

TRACEY: Yeah, go home to mummy, you sad perv.

EN MASSE: This is a customer announcement. The post office is now closed.

TRACEY: Bollocks to this, I'm off.

STACEY: Yeah, fuck this for a game of soldiers.

VIV: Me too.

BETH: (to Viv) Fine, that's just fine. I'll just have to come back tomorrow. Without you.

CRO-MAG: I didn't get the Christmas stamps. Me mum'll kill me.

Exit all but 'Anneka'

'ANNEKA': (to audience) How's my hair? Well today, the citizens of Leatherhead have raised a magnificent five pounds for the afflicted. Tomorrow I'll be in…

Enter Stacey

STACEY: Dad, It's time to go home now. Dad!

Exeunt

West Yorkshire Fire and Rescue Service

On the occasion of his ninth decade,
My great grandfather was lucky
Enough to have eighty candles
Upon his birthday cake.
And when the magnificent flicker
Turned into a blaze,
He proved luckier still:
To have sired a member of
The fire brigade.
For a lung had been lost
Beneath the pit head.
That was not so lucky.

Notes on a hangover

What's died in my mouth?
Who's coshed my head?
Why did they do it?
Do they want me dead?
What was I drinking?
Where did I go?
What did I do there?
Does anyone know?

I have a tendency to pursue what may
be lost causes

Last stand of the unknown shipping clerk

The man was slim and slightly stooped
On the sidewalk of the sodden street.
His mask-like face, clamped by irons;
Toned sepia and scored by dust,
Whispered faint scatters of confetti
Into the horizontal rain.

It seemed that he could scarcely stand
The weather seeped into his skin.
As I passed him on my way to work,
Some citizens had gathered round.
When I returned at half-past five
He lay in pulp upon the ground.

Save for his crumpled trilby hat;
A name inside, under the brim.
But as I stopped to take a look,
A dustcart drove away with him.

Headless horseman

The sky glows as if burning in the sodium glare
Of streetlights that stand sentinel
On the devil's road, an anthracite serpent
Constricting the capital in mirthless coils,
Upon which we gallop a relentless pace.
Towns flash by at a hundred and ten,
Infernos blazing in the November night
Which roars with the thunder of stampeding wagons
Ploughing salt into the conquered ground.
Cold sweat on my hands, the coachman drives on,
He spares neither horses nor mercy for those
Scattered to fate by his furious charge
As he spits vitriol at the laggards and meek

Obstacles in his race to the underworld.

In the jaws of the dog days

She arrived with the first test of summer and
It seemed that every day I would find
Her badly pitched tent of matted fur
Sprawled across the baking flagstones,
Seared by the blue heavens, cloudless
But for the glaucoma that fogged eyes

Never to see the first Match of the Day.

The children came again today

It was Jim O'Reilly who said that I should get a dog. At first I made excuses and told him that I had never really been much of an animal person, and that besides, Amy was frightened of just about any dog, especially those big enough to be much use here. But then I saw that Jim was looking at me with concern. I caught myself, and remembered that, of course, I no longer had a daughter. Jim said that it takes a while to remember this sort of thing and that his brother's bitch had just about weaned her litter and that it would be no trouble at all if he made an enquiry. I mumbled that it maybe it was a good idea and thanked him and he said he would call in the week and that I should watch out for myself.

After he drove off in his truck, I stood there for a second before I shut the trunk, wondering whether he meant to call by telephone or by truck, but I figured that there wasn't much chance that I'd be anywhere else but home, if that's what I could call it yet.

Just about a year's gone by since, and I can just about remember that Amy and Janine are dead. Most of the time, that is. And it's not how you would think; I don't wake up in the middle of the night and call their names, or anything like that. It'll be in the evening when I've been motivated to cook dinner, instead of something, anything, between two slices of bread, and the stew's bubbling on the stove and everything is warm and cosy, despite that dusk is coming down about the eaves, and I feel warm and fuzzy until I realise that I only needed to set one place for dinner. That's when it hit me, when I'd made enough food for the family and I would share it with the Colonel as the drizzle began to glumly fleck the windowpane.

Whenever I talk about my family, which is as little as possible, it's always Amy first, and then Janine. That's the order in which I would have dragged them from the wreck, if I hadn't been pinned, unconscious, behind the steering wheel.

The accident happened in the most banal of circumstances. We had just set out for Amy's little league game when just as we were about to turn onto the main road, some stupid kid ran out into the road, firing a toy gun. I slammed on the brakes, but the Camaro behind (driven I fancied by the stupid kid's even more moronic elder brother) didn't, and punted us out into the path of an on coming juggernaut. The stupid kid got way without even a scratch.

And it's the kid that haunts my dreams. Not that I don't dream of Amy and Janine, but sometimes I only know when I wake up to find my pillow damp with tears, but when I wake up screaming in the middle of the night, it's always the kid who's come to me, and lately he's been bringing his friends.

At first he didn't wake me up. I'd see him running down the pavement with a hoop for some reason, or riding a bike that had streamers flowing from the handlebars. Then I'd become overcome with a creeping dread and I'd try to warn him, I'd yell at him to slow down, to stop, but he wouldn't, and as he would get swallowed up by the ground, I'd realise that he couldn't hear me, that I was pinned behind the wheel in a car wreck and that I could barely breathe, let alone raise my voice to warn some stupid kid in the street.

And then I'd wake up, practically mummified in the bedclothes, out of breath through suffocating myself.

So just about a year had passed and I found myself talking to Jim again. I'd come to buy groceries and he to get a truckload of feed. I'd got to know Jim a little by this point so he said did I want to get a coffee at Marcy's? Sure thing, I said, so off we went. We sat down in a booth and Jim said that the cherry pie sure looked tasty. I bet it does, I said, all I ever see you buying is feed and sometimes I get to wondering whether you sit down to eat with the horses. More often than not he said, and sometimes he thought that he might as well move into the stables and rent the house, since Cathy's gone he said and looked sad. That's when Marcy said why the long face and Jim reckoned that he better have a slice of that pie.

A while later the sky began to darken and Jim said that he better get back before the weather closed in, but I stuck around to send a few emails. My agent appreciated that I might still be in mourning, but made a suggestion that I might try to write myself out of it. And you know I'd been thinking along those lines. They told some good stories round these parts, and even though some of them were probably as long as the prairie horizon I'd made a tentative note to maybe talk to some of these wizened cowpokes and see if they'd like to get their stories in a book. And if they agreed, I was sure that I'd hear about a farmer who moved in with his livestock and shared their oats and probably more besides.

I was wondering whether to tell my agent that his bankable (his word) horror writer was planning to go country when Marcy said that it was looking like heavy weather and they were sending the kids home from school as some of them had thirty or more miles to go home, and that I should probably go home and batten down the hatches. She was probably right (I always bowed to the locals' advice) so I paid my check. As I crossed the road to my car, I looked up at the sky and thought that it didn't look too bad, but the weather here could change in an instant, that it could equally be a violent thunderstorm as a drop of rain. Then again, in 15 minutes time the clouds could blow over to leave a peaceful blue autumn sky.

As I got closer to home, I reckoned that I'd been right to heed Marcy's advice. The sky had got lower and lower, until it almost seemed to brush the car roof and to have dipped the maize fields in grey watercolour, and the grass verges bristled angrily in the advancing wind. I couldn't get home soon enough and was looking forward to heating up a pan of pork and beans and eating it with the Colonel at my feet, passing the empty plate down for him to lick.

Then as I pulled up to the house, something caught my eye by the front door. Something dead, in pieces. It could have been a deer, brought down by a puma, but as I got out of the car and took a closer look, I retched.

It was the Colonel or what was left of him, and already cold. I turned away and vomited. The corpse bore little resemblance to a German shepherd. Irregular lumps of flesh, bone and fur, and were it not that the flesh was so obviously not burned, it looked like it had been hit by a bomb. With the tang of bile livid at the back of my throat, and my tears dried up by rage, I took a shovel from the shed and as the wind whipped up and threatened to claw the shirt from my back, I began to dig a hole by the edge of the woods.

By the time I stood in the hole and saw that the edges came as high as my waist I thought that I was just about done, something that also seemed to apply to my aching back, and my hands, palms blistered on the shovel and knuckles raw from the sides of the grave. I caught my breath and wept.

I decided that I might as well just shovel up the Colonel's remains and carry him to the grave that way. And it was as I deposited the first load into the grave that I noticed that something was seriously amiss. Though they were now matted with blood, before it died this dog had white paws. Colonel's, like most of his fur, were brown. And although it was far from appropriate I burst into rich peals of laughter; it wasn't the Colonel after all, he was ok, it was all going to be all right. I finished burying the unfortunate and anonymous dog and, in the bare soil I planted at twig that I broke off a nearby beech. I hoped that it would grow into a tree.

I washed my hands in the outside sink, took my groceries from the car in one arm and reached for the house keys. But as I walked up to the porch I was shocked for the second time that afternoon. Adjacent to the lock, the doorframe had been smashed and evil looking splinters stabbed out of the wood. Then a thought chilled my blood. In the excitement of realising that the mauled dog was not the Colonel, it had not occurred to me to check on him, it had not occurred to me that I should have heard his barked welcome the instant that I pulled up to the house.

I thought of you as a cat

I thought of you as a cat, curled up
Purring on the sofa, moulting;
Or maybe a chinchilla. Anyway,
A small, furry animal to make fuss of.

But now you're a hedgehog. It's true
You're cute and small, but prickly
When you curl yourself into a ball
No one can get close.

Matchwood

Your young men ran in packs,
Urinating on our feet with mocking grins
Before we were purged from the streets.
Exiled from your cities, fenced into ghettos,
We could only stand and watch
As your children tore away our babies
And dashed their brains out on the floor.
Spiny green overcoats were no match
For sticks and Start-Rite shoes.

We were few even then.
Our ancestors were felled in their prime,
Thousands were marched off
In bondage to conquer your empires,
Enslave and slaughter their kinfolk.
Few returned. Those that did were as corpses.
Now, on feast days, you bring your lollipop
Fingered families to gawk at us in display cabinets.
I believe you call them 'mausoleums'.
Those that were not shattered or drowned
Were dragged from their homes to be burned in public
Squares and flagellated in temples,
Forced to submit as commandments and idols
Were carved into their hearts and flesh.

And even though many of your kind
Now reject this legacy of horror,
Some of us have since succumbed
To poison gas and the acid bath.
Their ends were not swift.
But even as we hear the proclamations
Of your commanders and the curses
Of their mercenary lackeys:
Those dogs of war in yellow jackets
Rattling sabres in the grimy dawn,
We will stand our ground.
Defiant to the last with hearts of oak,
What else are we to do?

A visit to my aunt

"…She was perfecting her wintery smile in a hard mirror tarnished with verdigris."

"Oh, do stop it Amy."

I started as my great-aunt Mary raised her spectacles to her face, squinted at them as if they were an unpleasant curiosity, and with a look of exasperated resignation, slid them over her ears.

"Why do you insist upon reading that dreadful rubbish to me?"

I mumbled a protest that it hadn't been my idea, and in fact it was all of my mother's doing.

"Hmph. Typical, bloody typical. That girl never did stop meddling in affairs that were of no concern to her. Come on, let's have a look at it."

I passed her a slim volume of 'adult fairytales rewritten for the twenty first century' written by the current darling of the liberal media and shortlisted for several literary prizes. My aunt peered at it with distaste from within her easy chair.

"Dear me, I suppose she considers it to be improving."

I agreed that she probably did, and after prompting, agreed that a woman such as my aunt really wasn't in any need of improving.

"She hasn't had much success with you, has she?"

I stared at the floor between my scuffed German army boots.

"Well, good for you, that sort of thing causes nothing by misery. What do you read? That is, when you're not being told what to?"

I mentioned a small cache of Stephen King paperbacks that I kept under my bed where they cowered in fear of my mother.

"Each to their own I suppose, but give me a good murder any day, with lots of blood and a handsome detective to solve the mystery. Now be a good girl and read me something exciting.

There's a bookcase in the conservatory. Turn right out of the door and left at the end. I'll be waiting for you."

Arm in arm, boredom and fear stalked the corridor of the care home, cloaked in sensible dressing gowns, bent over sticks and frames and heartily wishing they were somewhere else. I successfully located the conservatory and extracted a derelict volume of Ruth Rendell from a bookshelf that appeared to be in imminent danger of drunken collapse. Straightening up, I turned around and all but collided with the apparition that had silently snuck up behind me. A short, dishevelled man, long since past the prime of his life shuffled to himself from inside his pyjamas. Ouch. The apparition poked me in the ribs with a bony finger.

"I know you from somewhere."

Does he? I doubt it.

"I have to tell you something."

Really? What?

"It is hard to find the centre of gravity in a basset hound."

He seemed to be having some difficulty in finding his own centre of gravity, judging be the way his hands hung unsteadily in the air approximately six inches away from my chest. I ducked and wove around his flailing arms before fleeing, in a dignified manner, back to the relative sanctuary of room 14 where I related my fleeting encounter to my aunt. Her curiosity piqued by my heavy breathing and reddened face.

"You didn't let him grope you, did you?"

Er, no.

"Good, he would have, given the chance. It's all an act you know, he's fully compos mentis if he doesn't get his breakfast on time. He's nothing but a dirty old man, roaming the corridors, looking for a daughter, great-niece or grandchild to molest. Senile? Pah! He knows exactly what he's doing, causes the most dreadful scenes. Maybe you should have made him an offer, given him the heart-attack that he so richly deserves."

Men. We laugh with pity and contempt.

"So Amy, do you have a boyfriend?"

After the last one? No thanks siree.

"Are you?" Malicious pause. "A lesbian?"

I replied that I hadn't really given it that much thought.

"Maybe you should, while you're still young. I might have tried it myself, but it really wasn't the done thing in my day, quite beyond the pale. And then I married a fascist."

Great-uncle Bob a fascist?

"When he died we found an interesting cache of documents in his study. Including what appeared to be personal correspondence from Oswald Mosely himself. Baffled me somewhat, one learns to expect pornography, but not a shrine to the British Union of Fascists. Peculiar fellow your uncle, he wrote poetry to his dog. "

Why didn't I know this?

"If you had been there then I would have told you, I told your mother, but she's more concerned about her appearance than passing on the family history. Now, I've read that book before, but start with the first chapter and I'll think of some juicy tales to tell you."

It's 4am

It's 4am
The rain beats down
Like your salt tears

When you left town.

Man in a quandary

A thousand years I've walked this earth.
A thousand years since being summoned
To a body prone in the shifting sands,
An ancient tome clutched in his hand
At the perimeter of a circle inscribed in that sand,
Which within he lay, Vitruvian man.
I shook it. No reply.

A thousand years I've walked this earth.
A thousand years of rivers and streams
Flowing into the desert sea,
A thousand years spent wondering
As to my purpose,
His motives,
My dreams.

I can't even remember
Whether I'm
Supposed to be
Good
Or evil.

I've always had a strange relationship with both ends of a camera

Birds of Malta

There are no birds on Malta
But if you stand
On the ramparts of M'dina
You may see the tourist jets
(Of old, those silver birds)
On their finals to Luqa.

There is no birdsong on Malta
But in the middle seasons
You may hear the shotguns' report.

But the shotgun blast
Of the middle seasons and fireworks
Shake the parishes on festa days
The saint of Assisi has his too
On October the 4th.

There are no birds on Malta
But if you take your morning
Coffee at Caffe Cordina

You may observe a disgraceful pigeon.

Cowgirl

When he sluices the dust from his face
When he's scrubbed his crow's feet clean
Polished his buckle bright
Plucking the sad songs from his banjo
Drawing women like moths to a flame

He's still the handsomest man in the state.

Primavera

In the velvet darkness, a verdant musk
Saturated the air, narcotic with life.
As the salt slick sweat upon your skin,
Mapped a giddy tango.

And when the fingers of morning had smoothed
Away the lingering raven feathers of night,
The sun lazed in through bamboo slats

For the dust to dance in its radiant light.

Weybourne

The sea rushed to meet me
Like the excitement of a child or puppy
Or a lover. Bearing memories
Upon its waves;
Freighters upon the horizon
While above, beyond the cliffs
Sand martins and swifts
Darted and dive-bombed.
It seemed that the day
Was much too clement
For such warfare, and images

Of German Stukas.

Words

A rapier wielded by a maestro
The dull, bunched fists of a common thug
The fiery sting of a master's cane
The smooth caress of a lover's touch
A missile hurled from a righteous riot
A Ming vase dropped by a blundering clot
The last heartbeat of a dying man
Arrows drawn by a poisoned pen
The molesting paws of an unwelcome pest
As a drunk staggers into the night.

I fell down the stairs again today

Competency

I had always been told
That communication was an asset.
And they praised my skills
To such an extent
I didn't get the job,
As in their opinion

I would talk too much.

Stab

The long-suffering residents of Mansfield Lane, Lakenham, had long been accustomed to being woken up in the early hours of the morning. For nearly four years, the occupants of one of the houses had held regular noisy drinking sessions that would continue long into the night. But the events of 19 April 2005, were remarkable even by those standards. At about 5am, an ambulance arrived to find 16 year old Alex McAllister bleeding profusely from his left arm. His assailant had been a girl attending that night's party. The motive? He'd asked her for a cigarette. When upon her refusal, he'd said: "There's no need to be like that," her response had been to stab him in his left arm. But when wiser souls may have beaten a hasty retreat, McAllister merely laughed and told her to do it again. The girl acceded and stabbed him a second time. Clearly in need of a nicotine hit after his ordeal, McAllister again asked for a cigarette, and for his pains was stabbed for a third time. In his own words: "It was getting a bit much." McAllister was obviously made of stern stuff. For when the ambulance was looking for somewhere to park, he chased after it, shouting and swearing because he thought that it was going to leave him behind. He was then taken to hospital and treated for his wounds. He also declined to press any charges. But the plot thickens. In between the assault and the arrival of the emergency services a neighbour claimed to have seen McAllister being kissed by his attacker, who was saying that she was sorry and that she loved him. But in spite of this damning evidence, he denied allegations that she was his girlfriend, saying: "I don't know who she was. My girlfriend wouldn't stab me like that."

Dope

In the summer of 1993: Kurt Cobain was still alive; combat trousers were army surplus and New Labour hadn't yet been invented. I was fifteen and smoking a joint on the school field. Quite how we got away with it, I'm unsure.

Cannabis was rather more illegal than is today, and one of the teachers used to eat her sandwiches in her car less than a hundred metres from where we sat in a huddled circle, negotiating over who was to provide the ingredients for our lunchtime refreshment, before playing loose and critical attention to whoever had been delegated the task of skinning up. It doesn't quite seem credible that the teachers had no suspicions about what we got up to in the hour between physics and double art. But maybe they thought we were just having a crafty fag, and were preoccupied chasing after those who caused much consternation to the local residents by flocking down to St John's Close whenever the bell went. That, or they were deliberately turning a blind eye.

Let's face it: we weren't troublemakers. We were from nice middle class homes, with parents who were teachers, scientists, lawyers and suchlike. As long as we didn't skive classes or act up when we were in them, pretty much everything else was up for negotiation. A kid called James drank half a bottle of whisky on the last day of term, and passed out on his desk. Nothing serious came out of that. It seems more than a little hypocritical that we, the well-mannered offspring of the professional classes were able or allowed to get away with what a council estate tearaway would have been at the very least suspended for. But I guess it proved a valuable lesson in the art of getting away with it. If you keep up appearances then you have to do something seriously shady to get busted.

Someone did get busted in the end though. But he was a dealer. Pete, the first kid in our year to get into the Pixies, had come to the conclusion that selling dope was by far the easiest way to supplement his meagre allowance. For £7 a teenth he'd sell you a nasty little lump of resin that scorched the back of your throat and put the shutters up to the rest of the world. This went on for a few months until he was rumbled after some sap failed to conceal his stash properly, and had to tell his mum where he'd bought it. And although they let him come back under guard to take his

GCSE exams, Pete ended up on a downward spiral to Hellesdon hospital and was last seen stamping a pigeon to death outside Next.

The thing was, one of dope's great attractions was that it was somewhat easier to get hold of than drink because, although the outlets were harder to find, drug dealers have generally less scruples than licensed premises. So long as you have the money and don't look like a grass then it's yours. It's also more economical, easier to conceal and you're less likely to vomit in unfortunate places.

The well

Thank you for calling the hotline
For further information please press "one" now.

You may ask any questions you like,
Although we regret that the answers are classified.
For further information please press "one" now.

You are not a prisoner and may leave
Whenever you feel able to.
The whys, whens, wheres and whats
Of your existence can only be answered
By yourself alone.
If you are curious, please press "one" now.

You may have already noticed that
During your stay
You will not physically feel hunger,
Thirst or the need to evacuate your bowels.
Please press "one" at your leisure.
You have all the time in the world.

We regret that we are unable to provide an outside line:
Though please be assured that your friends,
Family and colleagues,
Should you have any,
Will not notice your absence. Equally,
Your return will cause no surprise,
It will be as if you'd never left.
If you are here, please press "one" now.

Thank you for calling the hotline.
We hope that we have been of assistance.
Please call again at any time.

The flu (after John Donne)

I have the flu and feel like shit
Yet apportion no blame, though I know it
Infected you and now ails me,
This is not how I wished that things would be.
My body sweats, I never should
Have caught this fever in your neighbourhood.
For what at first glance looked so fine,
Is a quicksand castle, no grand design
I cannot be yours, neither you mine.

I'm sure you'll lead a happy life
Far away from me, my blight and strife.
This flu is you and I as this
Untidy bed and chaotic desk is
(I should say "are," but Donne did not.)
Sometimes I'm chilly, at others hot,
I hope this flu does not kill me,
For I'm melodramatic, can't you see?
Not to be taken too seriously.

Cruel and sudden, get flu hence
For in self-pity, I claim innocence.
I'm not bad, just careless and slack,
I trod on life's tail, and it bit me back.
Now flu triumphs for I am ill,
I was never strong, and now weaker still,
In no fit state for more swordplay.
And I wager that soon I'll hear you say
I wasn't worth it anyway.

Iceskating

It is the first Saturday before Advent. The city is teeming with a nascent hope and promise on a brisk November afternoon. The Christmas lights have been lit for the past week and even the junkies outside the Guildhall are wearing floppy red hats like so many little helpers, though I don't wish to dwell on whom their Santa might be. The shops are pillaged to the jingling of sleigh bells and cash registers. Tom Cratchit goes unnoticed as Tom Cratchits do and, outside the library, the ice rink has opened.

My felt coat is warm and I wonder and hope whether I look like one of the Beatles in A Hard Day's Night as I skate surely across the ice as never before, my scarf wrapped snugly around my neck. I look over to where my companion, a young woman in a soft woollen hat, is adjusting her skates by the barriers. As she straightens her back, I glide up to her and take her hand in mine. As one, we glide and swoop around the rink, all glowing cheeks and smiles, before parting to circle around each other, inscribing Venn diagrams into the ice as we go. And soon we will ease the skates from our weary feet, and smile.

We will sit in rattan chairs at the rink side, under glowing patio heaters as hot chocolate and coffee, fortified with brandy, warms our hands and bodies, raising their temperatures to match our souls which, if they were not enclosed in vigorous flesh and blood, I fancy would glow like hot coals, radiating warmth, comfort, and light, to all that come near. We talk about the giddy present and the oncoming future, for the ice rink has worked its magic. Nervous questions have long since melted and been rendered obsolete in the thin winter sun, now sinking behind the rooftops. We know. And how we know. In the midst of Christmas and blazing winter fires, of long walks through frosty woods and up green mountains. We can barely dare to breathe, exhaling soft clouds of misty breath, which dissipate into the chill air like apprehension in a warm welcome.

And then I am woken. The metallic crash of a china cup on concrete paving shatters my reverie and brings me to my senses, their nerve endings abruptly exposed to the chilly breeze. And to reality where the paving slabs glisten with a discreet and inscrutable sheen, irregularly punctuated by the apathetic drizzle. The sky is a bruise, and a meagre shaft of washed out winter sunlight splits through a gap in the clouds like a bitter joke in a break up argument. Stupefied, my gaze wanders down to my coffee; now half drunk and wholly cold. The froth of steamed milk has solidified, and clumps of it float on the surface, sticking to the sides of the cup; a crust of algae on a neglected duck pond.

Dusk is falling, and the sky has turned a deep, opaque, petrol blue that I've never seen before, except in sets of coloured pencils. The next group of skaters emerge from the changing hut and stumble tentatively onto the ice. A pair of girls in their early teens shriek with laughter as they clutch onto the railings, their legs splaying like those of a newborn foal. I laugh too, not at them, but at my realisation that rather that the elegance, joy, and pure, nascent love, of my daydreams, any excursion that I might make onto the ice would inevitably result in my falling onto the ice, fingers grasping in vain for the railings and then swiftly but surely amputated by the skates of a girl not unlike the two that I am watching on the rink, their fur-trimmed hoods buffeting in the breeze as they complete their first unassisted laps. Or maybe the roles would be reversed.

Violent melodrama aside, I have the tendency to be rather more clumsy and awkward than not. Some days I can barely lift my coffee to my lips without spilling it down my front. So maybe I don't get the girl either. Or if I do, I spill the brandy-laced hot chocolate down her front, and I am left alone with my rapidly cooling coffee and the giggles of the girls in the fur-trimmed hoods. And it's thoughts like these that prevent me from getting anywhere with my life. Melodrama aside, of course.

My daydreams are frequent. They keep me company wherever I go, whether I am sitting in cafes, walking to the shops, or lying in bed when it seems like there's nothing to get up for, curtains drawn against the day. I am the leading actor in these plays, always biopics and I am always the hero, though in modest terms. Depending on recent stimuli, I may be a footballer, loyal to his home team even in the most desperate situations. I grudgingly agree to be transferred so that my fee will save the club from ruin, only to return in a few years to lead it back to glory (in these scenarios I always go back). Or I may be a decent working class lad, conscripted into a just war, where I acquit myself with honour and catch the eye of a senior officer who will mentor me in business upon peacetime. I may be a restauranteur, or a boxing champion who shuns the riches of the professional game in order to police his community and give hope and encouragement to the local youths. And yes, I get the girl more often than not.

By this time it is well and truly dark. The last frigid drops of mocha trickle down my throat like raindrops on a fogged up windowpane as I raise the cup to my lips. A galaxy of fairy lights shines brightly across the skating rink, empty of the skaters who have been usurped by a trio of scarlet-jacketed attendants who meander lazily across the ice, sweeping the surface and hustling frozen debris into the corners; and half a dozen patio heaters cast an eerie orange glow onto the coffee drinkers, the wicker chairs and the detritus of cigarette butts, empty sugar packets, and fallen sycamore leaves that speckle the ground in a grimy urban confetti.

Draped poignantly over the pale railings that encircle the skating rink, is a single candy-striped child's glove, lonely among the bustling evening throng of paroled school children and office workers that, in my detachment, remind me of nothing more than wriggling microbes in a Petri dish under a microscope. But then, when my gaze wanders back to the child's glove, and rests there for how long? It's maybe a minute or so, maybe longer before my humanity makes a sudden reappearance with a shiver that courses right the way through my body like a mild electric shock.

And with a jolt, the emotions that I had safely locked away burst from their filing cabinet. My nerve endings jangle-tingle like an electric razor, tears well up from under my eyelids and I am overwhelmed with an unbearable sadness that envelops me like a stricken vessel succumbs to the ocean deeps. At this moment I am that unknown child of the lost glove, alone in the dark, wailing for mother. Whether that child is truly lost, whether that child is snivelling because of the cold or chastisement for carelessness, or whether tucked up safely in a warm and loving home, I do not know.

War

When I was a small child, perhaps four or five years old, I knew there was war and I knew it was bad, but of its practice I had yet to learn. But an idea had formed in my head by unconscious means. I imagined the battlefield to be an alleyway of dusty redbrick walls that reached up to infinity, and between them a narrow strip of dirt just wide enough to aim a rifle. And stood eyeball-to-eyeball, with their backs up against these red walls, were the opposing armies of khaki soldiers, smoking, waiting for the bugle. And though I never heard it, the bugle would sound. And it must have sounded, for the soldier nearest to the alleyway's entrance would shoulder his rifle and shoot his enemy counterpart in the chest. Then as the stricken rifleman hit the dust, the soldier who was stood next to him would take aim at his comrade's assassin. And so he who took the first shot would be the second to fall dead, and the second to be avenged by his brother-in-arms as the third shot left the barrel. And so entire battalions would fall regiment-by-regiment, soldier-by-soldier, and if there was a victor then I never saw one, for the alley appeared to be infinite in length as well as height, and in carnage also.

How dare you

I reach the shop with not a moment to spare for the shop will soon be closing for the night, and I need time; time to take refuge, for the wind is now whipping the strands of rain across the road, like a cat o' nine tails onto the bleeding back of a miscreant sailor. Rivulets of water hustle down the gutters in a flurry of filth and I momentarily break into a run, which almost turns into a wild goose-step as I slip on a treacherous patch of rotting leaves, flailing as I try to keep my balance before stumbling up the steps to the automatic doors in which I catch my reflection. A drowning victim stares back at me from the glass panels, wet hair plastered to its face like strands of oily bladderwrack. But then the doors slide open and the apparition vanishes with a hiss and a moan.

Inside the shop all is calm and order. A regiment of strip lights clings to the ceiling, standing guard above the cigarette counter, which has been locked down for the night under dull metal shutters. Checkout operators sit stoically at their stations like barflies in an Edward Hopper painting as half a dozen late night shoppers stare through the plate glass windows, waiting for the storm to subside, like so many fishermen's wives scanning the horizon for the return of their menfolk.

And yet, as the automatic doors shut behind me with a slight thud, I wonder if I have brought part of the storm in with me, for the torpor of the Hopper painting is suddenly and brutally invaded by Edvard Munch's *The Scream*. The fishermen's wives turn away from their vigil as a short woman, fists pumping as she marches furiously towards the exit, yells "how dare you" over and over again. The stares are followed by shrugs and the wives return to their vigil at the window. Whoever "you" is, they are not in the building, as the security guards observe rather than pursue, and only to make sure that she leaves the building. As she does, buffeting me in her wake as she speeds past me. The doors whisper open and then thud shut again, fading her inquisition to a faint echo and there is no other sound but the hum of the refrigerators and, on the taxi rank outside, the rattle of a diesel engine as it splutters into life with the hacking cough of a bronchial old man.

Quickly, I go over to the booze aisle to get my whisky. As the checkout operator removes the security tag and I thrust a crumpled twenty-pound note in her direction, she smiles weakly in bewilderment and I shrug back in agreement. The only verbal communications that pass between us are mumbled thank yous and goodnights. In fact, during the few minutes that I have been inside the store, nobody has mentioned the woman's terrifying behaviour. Nobody that is, apart from one of the security guards as he whispers to his colleague while rotating an index finger around his right ear in the universal gesture that suggests insanity. All is quiet again. Too quiet.

As I leave the store, the storm mercifully seems to have blown itself out, and the rain has settled down into a steady drizzle. I screw my receipt into a ball as I go, and pause for a moment to drop it into a bin filled with the carcasses of ruined umbrellas, their black plumaged as ragged and wet as that of a pile of dead cormorants. And as I wonder who "you" might be, whether "you" is real or imagined, whether "you" might be cause, symptom, or demon. I hear the screaming again, coming from the war memorial at the back of the market. And as I look up I hear other voices as well, and it becomes evident that the woman has been intercepted by a police patrol that is urging her to calm down in gruff, yet understanding, tones. And years of experience have enabled them to do their job for her screaming has dwindled to a desperate, animal, sobbing that rises and falls with the peaks and troughs of her despair.

I walk on, not wishing to rubberneck.

The night cloaks me, enveloping my shivering body in its folds, wrapped tightly round my shoulders, and billowing in the wind as I struggle with the stubborn lock. Finally it gives, and my weight on the key slams the door open and I shuffle inside, hampered by the cloak which clings to my legs like a shroud. I push the door shut behind me, and the cloak brushes softly against the carpet as I trudge up the stairs and practically fall through my bedroom door onto the bed where the cloak falls softly over me and I slip into unconsciousness with terrible ease.

I'm sorry

I'm sorry that we don't appear
To speak the same language,
That we babble in different tongues.

I'm sorry that you got the house,
And that we ever bought it.

I'm sorry for what I never did,
Though our opinions may differ
As to what I lacked.
I'm sorry for my hurtful words,
And sorry that I let you drive me to them.
I'm sorry that your mother doesn't like me,
That I argued with your father.
And still sorrier that I didn't
Break his nose, leaving scarlet
Stains on his stuffed shirt.

I'm sorry that I feel the need
To make unnecessary apologies.

How terribly British of me.

The innocence of the jelly

I was five years old

I was five years old
When I stooped to pick
A daisy from the verge
It was but a moment
That I appeared in court.
I was five years old.

I was five years old
When I faced a thousand fists
Shaking like trees in a furious gale.
A thousand mouths contorted,
Mute with apoplexy.
Something was very wrong.
I was five years old.

I was five years old
When I was taken from this place
To another place; a wasteland
Red and angry as the faces.

The girl was five years old

She handed me a toy truck saying:
"It's hard to make lorries
But here's one." She left me
With no explanation,
Or was it a clue?
I have searched this wasteland
I am no longer five years old.
That is just a memory.

The man

The man has appeared to me in many guises. The first time was unexpected, as first times generally are. I was being hustled down the street in a gust of Arctic wind and fallen leaves when I started at the blaring of a car horn. I turned my head to see if whether I was being summoned by friend or foe, but it was neither so I turned back to my path. And there he was, bent and gnarled as the stick that took his weight, with an expression that lay somewhere between bewilderment and fury. I had not yet resumed my journey when he looked into my eyes, so I paused to hear him bear witness. He launched into a fierce tirade.

Misuse of the car horn was the subject of his sermon, which was long and rambling to the extent that I have forgotten it all but in essence. I felt that quite some time had passed before he drew enough breath for me to agree that the reckless use of such a device was nothing short of an utter disgrace. And then I said goodbye. And though that may appear to be sarcasm, or an insincere agreement to let me pass on my way without trouble, it was not, for a sudden noise or movement can startle me, and rob me of my composure for quite some time.

Travelling in hope

Although my flight does not leave until three o'clock in the afternoon, I arrive at the airport at sometime between eight and nine. The night before, I had conscientiously packed and repacked my luggage before ordering a taxi for the early hours of the morning so all I had to do was wake up, shower, and wait in the mist outside my front door at the appointed hour. The taxi driver was silent and the radio turned low as we surged through the empty streets while the newsreader spoke softly about some tragedy in a far-off place, the dark interior of the car relieved only by the green glow dashboard instrumentation and the sodium glare of the streetlights.

I drank acrid railway coffee as the first train of the day chuntered steadily towards London, and watched the world wake up as the sky changed from black to indigo to cobalt, before settling to a consistent pale grey silk that disappeared under the Victorian cathedral roof of Liverpool Street station where I was disgorged into the metropolis in the company of suited businessmen, and descended into the bowels of the earth to emerge at Victoria half-an-hour later, and thence to Gatwick.

I am in a good mood today. Of course I am on holiday, but I am seldom more at ease with myself than when travelling. I feel at home when in the transience of railway stations and airports, when seated in a train or plane watching the world go by whether twenty feet to one side or thirty thousand feet below. I gaze at departure boards as all of humanity swarms underneath bound for Moscow, Dubai, Santiago and Paris. Extended families clustered around caravans of baggage trolleys checking in for the evening flight to Lahore. Experienced business travellers with hand baggage only alight from the red-eyes from Athens and Dusseldorf, the cluster of anxious reception committees at arrivals clutching signs welcoming Herr Maier, Monsieur Lim and Ms Hernandez and bewildered immigrants taking the first steps of their new lives embracing their cousin who has found them work in Manchester or Glasgow. The names of the airlines: Aeroflot, Cathay Pacific, Libyan Arab and Alitalia resonate with hope and promise.

I even take time to wander round the airport shops and duty free. Somehow, everyday goods and brands take on an exotic sheen here. The Sony compact disc player and the bottles of Johnny Walker are more desirable in the bright plastic bags with Amsterdam emblazoned across them. This I why arrive early, to drink in this atmosphere so infused with potential. Indeed, I do believe that it is better to travel in hope than to arrive.

Late for work again

I remember one morning of a winter when the snow lay on the ground for weeks on end. At that time my morning walk to work passed through a park where, the evening before, a riot of school kids had compacted a slide in to the snow. I had watched them for a while as they scooted and skidded, whooping and laughing and taking the piss. Their happiness was infectious, and I felt that I could visibly see my spirits begin to rise like the mercury in a thermometer. But then I caught myself. These are days when it invites suspicion for a grown man to be seen watching children. I saw the mercury sink again, then shuffled home through the slush. This morning though, the school day was about to begin and the runway lay abandoned and ignored by the last stragglers of the morning commute, faces turned to the ground and huddled into collars and scarves.

Late for work again, I was crossing the park in the opposite direction, my footsteps matching those of the middle-aged businessman who was a couple of dozen or so paces in front of me. Our small convoy was approaching the bandstand when he stopped for a moment and, as I closed the distance between us, gave a shrug of his shoulders before deviating from his course to cut a diagonal across the grass and its carpet of snow. It took a second or so before I realised that he was making for the children's slide, at which point he stopped in order to plant his briefcase into a small heap of snow.

He then paced up and down the length of the runway, and I supposed that he making an assessment of its quality and dimensions. Evidently they were satisfactory, for he walked a few paces beyond the far end to a clump of dank rhododendrons and then turned around, rubbing his hands together in a way that suggested warming and anticipation. He stooped slightly with his head tilted forward, as if to get a better sight. Then, in a few strides, he ran towards the slide and launched himself along its length, arms outstretched for balance, before losing control at the end and falling into a heap of snow, laughing like the children before him. Then, after briefly examining his wristwatch, he rose to his feet, brushed the snow and ice from his coat, picked up his brief case with authority and strode off to the centre of town.

I tried to recall my childhood memories as I walked towards the park exit, but I had no carefree memories to look back on with affection. Not that I had a hard upbringing, far from it, but that I was so serious, shy, and awkward, that I seldom managed to break out from my shell and run with the wind.

My dinner, the volcano

Far below, a livid crater
Scorches all that venture close
A furnace bright with seething magma
Alive and yet deadly both
Bulging now to burst its borders
As seeds from a ripened pod
An altar fit for sacrifices
To placate a hungry god.

Please don't fight

The gathering evening gloom casts a pall of dread over the bare windswept parking lot where I sit, hunched into a corner, in the back seat of my mother's car. In the months and years to come I will become used to this, the minutes that seem like hours that seem like days as we wait for my father to pick me up for the weekend. Grey weeds limp against grey asphalt. A monochrome silence creased only by sad flecks of drizzle as they splat against the grubby window while I pick at the frayed brown nylon upholstery, and occasionally punctuated by my monosyllabic replies as my mother asks me about my new school and if I've made any friends. But mostly we sit and wait, my head turned away so as not to catch sight of her face. I can't cope with other peoples' sadness. My own, that's none of your business, but seeing a five-year-old girl bawl her eyes out at an ice cream cone ruined on the sidewalk, it makes me well-up inside. The thing is, if I had the money, I could buy a new cone for that little girl and her sadness would be gone as swiftly as it began. I don't know what to do when grown-ups cry.

I turn my head away when I see my father too. I don't want to see the sadness in his eyes either, and miss the aura of calm reassurance that used to answer my incessant questioning and send me off to school with a hearty yet tender pat on the back. I also fear his new moustache that bristles ominously on his top lip, as I now fear the twenty-minute walk to and from school, along strange streets with the older kids and younger kids and the fat, weird and smelly kids who desperately want to be my friend, but whom I avoid with still greater vigour than the bullies. I'd rather have my lunch money stolen and go hungry than be marked as one of them. That way lies certain death.

I can hear my mother's breath quicken as the receding sun turns the parking lot a steadily darker monochrome. My father is late and there'll be hell to play. By the time his beat-up truck pulls through the dull wire gates, the last shreds of sunlight have all but disappeared over the horizon, and I hook my bag over my shoulder in preparation for a quick getaway. But my mother is quicker and the driver's door slams shut while I'm still trying to tell her that I love her and to have a good weekend.

"Where the hell have you been?" she yells as I cower in the twilight.

"Marie, I'm sorry, we had a problem at the plant. Needed to get it fixed before we left off."

I peer out at my father, tall and strong in pressed jeans, rodeo shirt and shiny brass buckle. Still looks his best on a Friday night. Despite all the hurt, he wants to show my mother that he hasn't let himself go, become a dirty old boar like some other kids dads', unshaven, drunk, some even child molesters, or so I've heard from Johnny Rivers.

"That's just you Frank, just you all over. That's all I got from you in twelve years of marriage. Excuses, excuses, excuses."

I sink lower in my seat, pulling my Yankees cap over my eyes. Please don't fight. I just want to eat burgers in front of the TV.

"Honey…"

"Don't you honey me. 'Honey, I gotta work late'; 'honey I gotta work weekends'; 'honey, I'm going out with the guys tonight'; 'honey we're on short time'."

"Marie…"

"No time, no money."

"I had to do what I had to do Marie. Jobs are going abroad, I'm lucky that I've still got one. Had to keep my hand in otherwise I'd be on welfare right now."

"Might as well have been for all the good it did us."

"Now don't say that, it ain't been easy for anyone."

"It ain't easy? It ain't easy? Try bringing up a kid when your husband's got no time or got no money. Don't talk to me about 'it ain't been easy'." She's angry now and even though I can't see her face I know only too well the wildfire that roars through her eyes. It's the Irish in her, my father used to say with a weak smile.

"But Marie…"

"No more. No more buts. No more 'honey', no more excuses or you'll never see Danny again."

I can't hold back any longer. Tears, time, or motion. Throwing open the

102

car door I bolt head long at my father and fling my arms around his waist, inhaling the comforting, familiar smell of his aftershave.

"No. Don't. No more. No more. No more fighting." I choke between sobs. Silence. I turn to my mother, her face a crazy amber in the streetlights' sodium glare. My father puts his arm around my shoulder and it feels hard, unyielding.

"It'll be alright, son."

"Promise?"

He winces in lieu of an answer and my mother's face collapses into remorse. And as she makes her apologies and goodbyes, I turn around and see the rough plaster cast on my father's right hand.

The haunting

I know that you've stopped your drinking
But these days you don't seem to eat,
You don't touch your toast, you're becoming a ghost;
Your face has gone white as a sheet.

You flinch when I reach for your hand.
Can't run my fingers through your hair,
You don't make a sound, as if you've gone to ground;
Sometimes it seems like you're not there.

You never answer the phone now
You won't even open the door,
You're hurting your friends and I can't make amends;
Don't think I can take any more.

You lie in your bed like the marble
On a tomb sinking into the ground,
You give me a fright when you creep out at night;
Never making a sound.

Sugar mice

I never hear your tiny footsteps
As they pad away in the dead of night.
And seldom too, when you return
With a sorrowful and tiny gift,
Imploring eyes and a plaintive mew,
"What have I done that is so wrong?"
I comfort you with loving fuss; I try
Not to stroke your fur the wrong way,
Those golden threads that weave into the carpet.
I never know quite why you start
And run away from my affections.
And why sometimes, when all I seek
Is to hear you purr; you take a swipe.
One cut among a thousand,
Language I wish I knew.

A pitch into the void

Within hours, you will leave for the station
For the very last time. We shall embrace
In the hallway while the taxi
Meter runs and a plume of exhaust
Melts into the November gloaming
Like spectral lovers at ease.

I will learn sometime later from a mutual friend
That you will be married to a patrician
Who will take care of you
In the way that he knows best.
Though I will not receive an invitation
Inscribed in gold leaf,
I may attend your wedding regardless.
And whether by my own will
Or by that of a tuxedo's strong arms,
Leave before the party ends although
I will not have caused a disturbance,
Know the desire that ejects me,
Nor whose feelings must be spared.

And while you peer from the bars
Of your gilded cage,
I will imagine a fortune
And wander the earth in a daydream,
An Amex tramp,
Home no more than a word.
My affairs as foreign to me as I to them.

But one day, and quite by accident
We will meet again in a daze
Of recognition, roaming the off-season streets
Of a European capital, cleansed
By tears and drizzle
In a scene half remembered
From a subtitled film, as I make my way
Between sopping rhododendrons
In a wet British park.
Those, at least, are real.

Acknowledgements

When my big brother Ben died it affected me more deeply than I would ever have imagined; and having this book to focus on has been such a positive way of dealing with that. One of my first instincts was to gather all of Ben's writing together to share with family and friends, but at the time I didn't imagine what a big project it would become.

Ben's friends have been truly amazing – they've been so welcoming that I really feel I've inherited a whole group of new mates; not to mention that for each job that's needed doing at least one of them (and usually several) seems to be an expert in that area. So many people have given up so much of their time for this to make it such a great tribute to Ben.

In particular I'd like to say a big thank you to:

- My Mum, Glenys, for supplying a venue (and pies) for our early meetings, and for making the whole thing possible.

- Mark for the brilliant pictures, and for trusting me with his sketchbooks.

- JB for the idea that became *songs in the key of ben*; and for organising and producing the CD, as well as all the cover artwork for the CD and the book.

- Liz for being an important presence at each stage along the way, and for keeping us all on track.

- Everyone in the bands who contributed – I love all the songs, particularly how each one is so different, but they all really capture something of Ben in them.

- Owen for a memorable weekend at the Sickroom.

- Sam for sharing his skills for the layout of the book, and for asking all the questions that no one else had thought of.

- Rob, Angela, Abi, Mikey and Mel, for being so enthusiastic, and for supplying all sorts of great ideas along the way.

- Charlene and Annie for taking charge of the PR and the launch party.

- Joe for setting up the website, www.birdsofmalta.com

- George Szirtes for giving us some valuable advice early on, and for agreeing to write a foreword.

- My Dad, Martin, for his persistence in taking photos of Ben and I at every possible opportunity.

- Mia for being so encouraging when we first discussed the idea of the book.

I'm sure Ben would be cringing at the idea of publishing his work, but I'm also sure he would secretly be very pleased at how it has turned out.

Ellen